ACCLAIM FOR COLLEEN COBLE

"Coble's atmospheric and suspenseful series launch should appeal to fans of Tracie Peterson and other authors of Christian romantic suspense."

—LIBRARY JOURNAL REVIEW
OF TIDEWATER INN

"Romantically tense, but with just the right touch of danger, this cowboy love story is surprisingly clever—and pleasingly sweet."

—USATODAY.COM REVIEW
OF BLUE MOON PROMISE

"Colleen Coble will keep you glued to each page as she shows you the beauty of God's most primitive land and the dangers it hides."

—WWW.ROMANCEJUNKIES.COM

"[An] outstanding, completely engaging tale that will have you on the edge of your seat . . . A must-have for all fans of romantic suspense!"

—THEROMANCEREADERSCONNECTION.COM
REVIEW OF ANATHEMA

"Colleen Coble lays an intricate trail in *Without a Trace* and draws the reader on like a hound with a scent."

—ROMANTIC TIMES, 4½ STARS

"Coble's historical series just keeps getting better with each entry."

—LIBRARY JOURNAL STARRED
REVIEW OF THE LIGHTKEEPER'S BALL

"Don't ever mistake [Coble's] for the fluffy romances with a little bit of suspense. She writes solid suspense, and she ties it all together beautifully with a wonderful message."

—LIFEINREVIEWBLOG.COM
REVIEW OF LONESTAR ANGEL

"This book has everything I enjoy: mystery, romance, and suspense. The characters are likable, understandable, and I can relate to them."

—THEFRIENDLYBOOKNOOK.COM

"[M]ystery, danger, and intrigue as well as romance, love, and subtle inspiration. *The Lightkeeper's Daughter* is a 'keeper.'"

—ONCEUPONAROMANCE.NET

"Colleen is a master storyteller."

—KAREN KINGSBURY,
BESTSELLING AUTHOR OF
UNLOCKED AND LEARNING

A
HEART'S
DANGER

Also by Colleen Coble

A
HEART'S
DANGER

COLLEEN
COBLE

THOMAS NELSON
Since 1798

NASHVILLE   MEXICO CITY   RIO DE JANEIRO

Published in Nashville, Tennessee, by Thomas Nelson. Thomas Nelson is a registered trademark of HarperCollins Christian Publishing, Inc.

Thomas Nelson titles may be purchased in bulk for educational, business, fund-raising, or sales promotional use. For information, please e-mail SpecialMarkets@ThomasNelson.com.

Scripture quotations are from *The Holy Bible*, King James Version.

Library of Congress Cataloging-in-Publication Data

Coble, Colleen.
  A heart's danger / Colleen Coble.
    pages ; cm. -- (A journey of the heart ; 3)
  Summary: "On the brink of war with the Sioux, a young woman risks everything to expose the betrayal threatening the man she loves. Christmas is coming, and the air at Fort Laramie has turned cold . . . but relations with the Sioux have turned colder. As tensions between soldiers and natives approach a tipping point, Ben Croftner and Jessica DuBois prepare a trap for Rand Campbell. Bitter from rejection and backfired plans, Croftner has enlisted the help of Rand's new fianc?e to keep Rand from ever returning to Sarah Montgomery...for whom his heart clearly still yearns. Sarah is simply trying to move on with her life at Fort Laramie, but doing so under the watchful eyes of both Campbell—the manwhose love she craves—and Croftner—the man whose lies have cost her everything. Will Rand fall victim to the conspiracy and go through with his wedding? Or will he declare his love for Sarah and make good on the promises that brought her into the rugged western territories?"—Provided by publisher.
  ISBN 978-0-7180-3166-4 (softcover)
  1. Man-woman relationships--Fiction. 2. Triangles (Interpersonal relations)--Fiction. 3. Frontier and pioneer life--West (U.S.)--Fiction. I. Title.
  PS3553.O2285H427 2015
  813'.54--dc23

                                    2014044567

Printed in the United States of America
15 16 17 18 19 20 RRD 6 5 4 3 2 1

In memory of my brother Randy Rhoads, who taught me to love the mountains of Wyoming, and my grandparents Everett and Eileen Everroad, who loved me unconditionally. May you walk those heavenly mountains with joy.

A Letter From the Author

Dear Reader,

I can't tell you how excited I am to share this story with you! It's the first series I ever wrote, and it will always be special to me because writing was how I dealt with my brother Randy's death. You'll see a piece of my dear brother in Rand's character throughout this series. These four books were originally titled *Where Leads the Heart* and *Plains of Promise*. They haven't been available in print form for nearly ten years, so I'm thrilled to share them with you.

When my brother Randy was killed in a freak lightning accident, I went to Wyoming to see where he had lived. Standing on the parade ground at Fort Laramie, the idea for the first book dropped into my head. I went home excited to write it. It took a year to write, and I thought for sure there would be a bidding war on it! :) Not so much. It took six more years for a publisher to pick it up. But the wait was worth it!

This series seemed a good one to break up into a serialization model to introduce readers to my work. Even in my early stories, I had to have villains and danger lurking around the corner. :) I hope you enjoy this trip back in time with me.

E-mail me at colleen@colleencoble.com and let me know what you think!

Love,
Colleen

ONE

❦

EARLY MARCH 1866

The morning sun glinted on the patches of remaining snow as Sarah Montgomery hurried along to the Sioux encampment. Soldiers practiced in the big parade ground lined by fort buildings, and the sound of bugles pierced the cold air.

She rounded the last building and stopped in her tracks. An exodus of the Indian encampment was in full swing. Horses pulling travois of dismantled teepees

❦

and belongings packed the road north. She searched
the throng for her friend Morning Song. There she was
on a big buckskin. Sarah waved and called her name.

Morning Song slid from the horse's back and met
her at the end of the procession. She was fully recov-
ered from the beating she'd taken from the hands of
her so-called "husband" in November.

Sarah hugged her. "What's happening? Where are
your people going?"

"We go to meet up with Big Ribs. The elders were
all too ready to talk of war after what Ben did." There
was no lilt, no joy in Morning Song's voice. "I cannot
stay here. Ben will find me if I remain."

The wind blew across the parade grounds, and
Sarah shivered. "But you're safe here. The soldiers will
protect you now."

Morning Song released her and stepped back. "I
must go with my people. Thank you for all you have
done for me, Sarah. I will never forget you."

A lump formed in Sarah's throat. "That sounds
like good-bye."

"I hope to see you again, my friend, but . . ."
Morning Song looked down. "I fear our people will
be at war soon."

"We will always be friends, Morning Song."

The young woman nodded. "My mother waits. I must go." She hugged Sarah again, then pulled herself up onto the horse's bare back and rode to join the line of moving horses.

Sarah watched them go with a profound sense of sadness. At least Morning Song was out of Ben's clutches. When she came back, perhaps her spirit would have healed from his abuse.

When Sarah turned, she nearly ran into Rand Campbell. His big hands came down on her shoulders to steady her, and she looked up into his handsome face. A muscle twitched in his square jaw, and there was no sign of his dimples. She found it hard to read him these days.

She stepped away. "Sorry I nearly ran you down."

His arms fell to his sides. "A tiny thing like you couldn't knock me down. Are you okay?"

She nodded. "I'm sad to see her go, but at least Ben won't be able to touch her." With a parting smile, she turned toward the quarters she shared with Jacob and Amelia.

The impermanence of her situation gnawed at her. Isaac Liddle seemed to care about her and her little brother Joel, and she suspected he would propose soon. Even though she craved a place of her own, there seemed no real haven for her. She still couldn't contemplate a future without Rand in it, but she had to figure it out. He was going to marry Jessica, and she had to accept it.

Snow flurries skated across the landscape as Ben Croftner crossed Fort Laramie's parade ground and stomped toward the Sioux encampment. The wind poked icy fingers through his thick coat and tried to tear the hat from his head, but he barely noticed the glowering clouds overhead. He had more important things to do this morning than worry about the weather.

Just let those savages try to stop him from taking Morning Song. His fingers curled into his palms with the desire to smash a face or two. Although the face he really wanted to destroy was Lieutenant Rand Campbell's. As he walked in front of the officers' quarters, someone called his name. He turned to see a red-haired woman waving to him. Her pale skin was flawless, and her full lips turned up in an alluring smile.

Her lashes fluttered in a come-hither way. "Mr. Croftner."

She certainly was beautiful, if you liked the type. Cool and remote. He stopped at the steps and smiled at her. "At your service. I believe I've heard of you. You are Miss Jessica DuBois, correct?"

"I am. Won't you come in, Mr. Croftner? I think we have something in common."

He allowed his gaze to sweep over her until she flushed. "And what would that something be?"

She lifted her chin and her smile evaporated. "We both want to keep Sarah Montgomery away from Rand Campbell." She took a step back toward the door. "Won't you join me for some tea?"

Morning Song could wait. He followed her inside to a large parlor with a soft flowered carpet on the wood floor. Delicate tables flanked a horsehair sofa and three chairs completed the furnishings. Garden pictures and gold sconces adorned two walls while the fireplace dominated the third. The dining room was through an arched doorway.

A young, attractive black woman hovered in the doorway, and Jessica glanced at her. "Bring us some tea, please, Rose."

Rose nodded and walked out of his sight.

Jessica indicated one of the chairs. "Have a seat, Mr. Croftner." When he shrugged out of his coat and sank into the comfortable chair, she settled on the sofa and arranged the folds of her green dress. "I have a plan."

As she explained her plan, he began to smile. It was superior in every way to his own. Sarah would learn his vengeance was terrible.

He crossed his legs. "Tell me more."

Rand paused with his group at the North Platte River Bridge. He could see miles in all directions across the plains so it should be safe for the night. He waved to his brother Jacob. "We'll spend the night here so we're ready to restring wire for the telegraph in the morning."

Jacob nodded and dismounted. He was shorter than Rand and stockier, with dark-brown hair and eyes, but no one was able to miss the clear resemblance between them. He ordered the soldiers to set up camp. Rand pulled the saddle off Ranger and broke some of the ice in the river so the horses could drink. He heard a shout and looked up to see a group of fifteen Sioux, faces painted, charging across the river toward them with shrill war cries.

Rand dove for his rifle. He lined the sight of the Henry up to his eye and trained it on a young warrior. Rand's finger paused on the trigger as he saw the youth's face. He was probably only fifteen, although he looked like he'd seen battle before—he had a livid scar running down one cheek. The boy stared at him defiantly as Rand put pressure on the gun's trigger.

Rand shook his head and lowered his rifle long enough for the boy to lift his spear in his hand and wheel around with a bloodcurdling yell.

"That there was a mighty big mistake, young feller." Rooster had seen the exchange. "You'll likely run into him again, and he won't be so charitable-like."

Rooster was probably right. But the warrior had reminded him of his youngest brother, Shane. The same careless free spirit. Rand just couldn't kill him.

The weather turned frigid and stayed that way. Days went by with no relief. Finally, the colonel announced a party at Old Bedlam. Rand tried to keep his distance from Sarah, but his gut tightened every time she swept by in Isaac Liddle's arms with her heart-shaped face turned up to his admiring glance. It was ridiculous to care that his friend was courting her, but Rand couldn't help the stab of jealousy that pierced his chest when he realized she'd likely marry Isaac.

Halfway through the party, a sentry rushed in. "Colonel, Spotted Tail is at the Platte!"

Colonel Maynadier jumped up and clapped his hat atop his thinning blond hair. "Raise the white flag and get my horse ready." He turned to Rand. "Lieutenant, I hate to drag you away from the festivities, but I need you to accompany me. We'll ride out to meet Spotted Tail and assure him of our good intentions. This is what I've been waiting and hoping for. He's been with Red Cloud. If Spotted Tail is ready for peace, perhaps Red Cloud is too."

Rand nodded. "I'll meet you at the corral, sir."

He followed the colonel and the other officers to the corral and got their horses. At least they were all dressed in their finest. It would show respect to the Sioux. The wind picked up as he swung atop Ranger's black back and the officers got into formation. They went out to meet the column of Sioux amassing over the rise. The wind carried the chanting to them.

Frowning, the colonel reined in his horse. "Sounds like a death lament."

Rand's gut tightened. Could Spotted Tail have died? He waited with the rest of the officers by the fort gate as the lament grew louder.

As the tribe drew nearer, he saw Spotted Tail's face drawn with grief, so the deceased wasn't the chief himself. Spotted Tail's horse dragged a travois with a shrouded body. Rand stared hard at the covered pack, but could see no hint of the victim. His fingers tightened on the reins as a messenger rode forward.

The Sioux warrior wheeled on his pinto, then went and stopped in front of Maynadier. "Chief Spotted Tail wishes to bury his daughter in the white man's cemetery. As Ah-ho-appa drew near death, she asked her father to bring her back here. Shall you honor this request?"

Rand inhaled and glanced over at his brother. This would hit Sarah hard.

The colonel inclined his head. "I would be honored to have his daughter in the white man's cemetery."

The warrior wheeled again and rode back to the

rest of the tribe. Rand couldn't hear what he said to Spotted Tail, but the chief urged his horse forward until he reached the colonel. He stopped close enough for Rand to see Ah-ho-appa's face.

Colonel Maynadier put his hand on his chest. "My heart grieves at your loss, my friend. I hope we can be at peace with your people now."

Tears welled up in Spotted Tail's eyes. "My heart is very sad, and I cannot talk on business. I will wait and see the counselors."

"Of course, my friend."

Rand fell in with the troops as they rode back to the corral. He didn't want to think of Sarah's grief. He shouldn't care so much about seeing her hurt, but heaven help him, he still did.

Back at the fort Jacob dismounted, then went to grab Ranger's halter. "You should be the one to tell Sarah."

TWO

The dance was long over by the time Rand got to the quarters where Sarah lived with Jacob and Amelia. Sarah sat stitching on quilting material in her lap when Rand strode into the parlor. The lamplight cast a soft glow over her glorious red-gold hair, and he caught his breath. She seemed to get lovelier all the time.

He cleared his throat. "Sarah?"

She looked up, and her green eyes widened as he stepped closer. "What's wrong?"

He'd never been able to hide his emotions from her. "I don't quite know how to tell you except to just say it." He took off his hat and raked a hand through his hair. "It's Ah-ho-appa. She's dead, Sarah. Pneumonia." He cleared his throat. "It's been a hard winter, not enough food. She was too weak to fight the lung infection."

Sarah stared at him. "No, not Ah-ho-appa." She reached up and grabbed his hand. "You must be wrong."

He squeezed her hand gently. "I'm sorry. I know you loved her."

Sarah shook her head. "There must be some mistake."

"There's no mistake. I saw her myself. Her father has asked for her to be buried in the soldier cemetery. He said she wanted to marry a soldier."

Sarah put her face in her hands and wept. "It's all my fault. If she hadn't been friends with me, she would have been content with her life. She would have married some young warrior who would have taken care of her."

Rand took her hands and drew her to her feet and into his arms. "I'm sorry, Sarah, but you did all you could for her. At least she didn't go through what

Morning Song did." Rand held her until her weeping was over. "The funeral's tomorrow. I'll take you if you want."

She lifted her wet face and nodded. "I must tell her parents how much I loved her."

Rand couldn't tear his gaze from her face. He'd always loved her compassion for other people. She was as beautiful inside as she was on the outside.

Several hundred mourners, consisting of Indians, off-duty soldiers, Colonel Maynadier, as well as Major O'Brien, who had arrived to take over command of Fort Laramie, crowded the parade ground at sunset for the funeral.

Sarah stood with Amelia in the cemetery. The scaffold beside them rose eight feet in the air. The soldiers had built it to hold the coffin to honor Ah-ho-appa. She couldn't tear her horrified gaze away from the heads and tails of two white ponies hanging from the structure.

Amelia, her dark hair tucked into a bonnet, looked that direction and grimaced. "Jacob said the ponies were her favorites, and they were killed to carry her into the afterlife. Their heads are pointed toward the rising sun." She gestured to a barrel of water. "That's to quench their thirst before they begin their ride."

Sarah shuddered and hugged herself. "It seems so barbaric."

She watched the ambulance bring the coffin. A mountain howitzer followed the ambulance. The post band played a solemn march as the Brulé Sioux with Spotted Tail circled the scaffold. Behind them marched most of the men of the garrison, and they formed a large square around the Sioux.

Her gaze touched on Isaac Liddle's open and honest face. She didn't know if she could ever feel as strongly about him as she did Rand, but she had to move on with her life. Somehow.

Officers transported the girl from the ambulance into the open coffin. Colonel Maynadier contributed a pair of gauntlets to keep Ah-ho-appa's hands warm. Rand added red flannel and Jacob put a pair of moccasins into the coffin.

The Sioux women walked to the coffin. Each whispered something to Ah-ho-appa and dropped a small gift inside. When the women were done, Sarah approached and gazed down into her friend's casket, built by the fort's carpenter. Her long, raven-black hair was braided with bright-red ribbons and lay draped over her shoulders and across the soft white elk skin that covered her.

Tears filled Sarah's eyes. "Good-bye, my friend." She dropped one of her brooches into the casket.

The colonel had arranged for both Sioux and Christian funerals. When the ceremonies were over, Sarah pushed through the crowd while Rand followed her.

"That was a nice thing to do," he whispered. "You've probably made a friend for life. I know it's hard for you, Sarah. It's all so different out here. You're used to activity and fun. It's pretty dreary confined to those small rooms all the time and never being allowed to go outside the fort. If the weather holds, how about going skating on the Laramie River tomorrow after worship services?"

Sarah nodded eagerly. Could he really want to spend some time with her, or was he just sorry for her?

"Jessica's been wanting to go for weeks."

Sarah's heart clenched. He didn't seem to hear her quick intake of breath as he offered his arm and escorted her back to her quarters. He'd made it clear where his loyalties were.

Sunday morning was bright and sunny, with the mercury hovering near twenty-five degrees though it was already March. Shouts of laughter and squeals echoed through the trees as Sarah laced her skates. She'd worn her warmest dress over a pair of Joel's trousers. Her brother was already out on the ice with his friends, and she smiled as he went zipping by with his blond hair flying in the wind.

Rand skated by with Jessica laughing up at him, and Sarah's heart squeezed. She got up and tucked her hands into mittens, then skated along the frozen surface of the river. She refused to let the circumstances spoil her day. Rand was going to marry Jessica, and she was determined to be fine with it.

She linked hands with Amelia and skated until Jacob came to claim his wife for a race. Her chest burned from exertion so she skated over to rest on a rock where she'd left her boots. The cold seeped into her skin after a few minutes, and she stood to warm up. There was a movement in the trees, and she squinted at the shadows.

Was that Jessica talking with Ben?

Something about their furtive behavior made her frown. She hadn't seen Ben since Ah-ho-appa's funeral, though she'd half expected him to accost her when she was out and about.

She wished she could hear what they were talking about. She stared at her skates. If she took them off, she might be able to move more silently in their direction. And where was Rand? Did he know his fiancée was with Ben?

She sat back down on the rock and untied her skates, then slipped them off. With her boots on, she moved as quietly as she could into the trees. The deep timbre of Ben's voice grew plainer as she leaned against a tree and strained to hear.

"I have the plan in place."

"I knew you were the right man to talk to." Jessica's words could just be made out over the wind. "I just want her out of the way. You won't hurt her, will you? Rand would never forgive me."

"Of course not. I only want the best for her myself."

Who were they talking about? Sarah wished she

dared to get closer, but she'd certainly be discovered. She tipped her ear toward the voices again.

"There's no great rush as long as you get it done," Jessica said.

"I'll get it done."

Footsteps came closer, and Sarah would be found if she lingered. If only she knew who they were talking about. Ben never wanted anyone's good but his own, so she feared for whomever he had in his sights next.

Rand glanced around the throng of people skating along the Laramie River. Jessica had been here just a few minutes ago, but she had disappeared, probably chatting with an admirer or two. Most of the soldiers envied him his fiancée, but he was beginning to weary of her constant jealousy about Sarah.

He saw a flash of blue on his left and turned to see Sarah skating toward him. Her green eyes held confusion, and she looked away when she saw him.

He skated to meet her and offered her his arm. "Care to skate with me? Jessica is nowhere to be found."

She bit her lip, then put her hand on his arm. "Of course."

Tendrils of her red-gold hair had escaped their pins and curled around her face. Maybe this hadn't been such a good idea, but he wanted to be polite since she was alone. They pushed off from the shore and joined the skaters in the middle of the river.

"Where's Jessica?" she asked after a long moment.

"I'm not sure. Maybe her mother wanted to talk to her."

"I don't think so."

He wasn't sure about the tone in her voice. Was that a challenge? "Did you see her?"

She shot a glance at him. "How well does she know Ben?"

He frowned. "Ben? I don't think she's met him at all."

She stumbled a little as she skated. "This is probably none of my business."

"It's a little late now. You saw her with Ben?"

She nodded and pointed with a mittened hand. "Back in the trees. They were talking about some plan."

"What plan?"

"I don't know. They didn't say, but they seemed to be well acquainted."

"I'll ask her about it. I don't like her spending any kind of time with Croftner. Maybe she doesn't know how many lies he's told and how he's wrecked my life."

She stopped in the middle of the river and grasped both his hands in hers. "Did he ruin your life, Rand? When you say it like that, I almost hear regret in your voice."

He wished he could forget about the way their hearts had seemed knit together by the Almighty. Forget the way her hair smelled and the way her lips tasted.

THREE

R and walked Jessica home in the twilight. Her cheeks were red from the cold, and her eyes sparkled. And no wonder. Nearly every soldier on the river had asked her to skate with him. He found he didn't have a speck of jealousy about it either.

Seeing Sarah with Isaac was another matter.

He stopped on her porch and pressed her hand. "I'll be gone tomorrow for a few days. I have wood detail."

She gave a pretty pout. "I'll miss you."

"Will you?" He stared down at her. Would she tell him the truth if he asked her about her conversation with Ben?

She tipped her head to one side. "Why are you looking at me like that? Do I have a smudge on my cheek?"

"I didn't know you knew Ben Croftner."

Her eyes widened. "I know everyone at this post, Rand. Surely you're not jealous. Papa asked me to deliver a message to Ben if I saw him. He was at the river so I did as my father asked. Was that wrong?"

"Of course not."

She was lying. He could see it in the way she cast her gaze at her boots, then looked back up at him with a calculated smile. She was so used to using her beauty to blind the men around her.

"Ben lied about me many times. I don't like him, and I don't trust him. I'd rather you never speak to him."

Color tinged her cheeks. "Very well, if you're going to pout about it. I'll tell my father to deliver his own message next time."

He squeezed her mittened hand. "Ben hurts anyone he comes in contact with. I don't want you to be one of his casualties."

Her expression cleared and she laughed, then went

up on her toes to brush a kiss over his cheek. "I love it when you're possessive. There's no one I want but you, Rand."

He released her hand. "I'll see you when I get back."

Her eyes were hurt and questioning as she turned to go inside. He had handled that badly. It wasn't her fault he hadn't realized there was more to a happy marriage than similar goals.

Two days later the afternoon sun warmed Rand's face as he led a detachment into the forest for wood. It had to be close to seventy degrees, and winter had given up without a murmur. Pools of water and mud stood where snowbanks had once piled.

They had four huge stacks of wood cut and were about to load it onto the mules and travois when loud yells sounded from down in the ravine to their right.

"Injuns!" Rooster grabbed his rifle and vaulted onto his horse.

There was a wild scramble as the rest of the men clambered onto their mounts and followed Rooster's mad charge.

"There's only three of them," Rand muttered as he fell into line. But the rest of the Sioux were hiding. As the main force leaped out from behind bushes and rocks, the charge of the cavalry faltered. Instead of three, there were at least twenty-five.

"It's a trap," Captain Brown shouted. "Retreat! Retreat!"

But Rand was in the front line, and retreat would invite an arrow in the back. He slid off his horse and flung himself down behind a boulder. He took aim and began shooting desperately, pushing away the reality of his own situation. He would get his company safely away, then he'd worry about how to get out himself.

Rooster wheeled around on his horse and fired at a group of Sioux crouching behind a rock. "Git out of there, boy! It's better to say 'here's where he ran' than 'here's where he died.'" When Rand kept firing, Rooster swore, then galloped away, still shouting for Rand to run.

Something bit into his flesh, and Rand grabbed his shoulder. His fingers dripped with blood when he pulled his hand away. A bullet? But these Indians just seemed to have bows and arrows. He heard another shot off to his left and felt a fiery sting on his left temple. Then darkness claimed him.

When Rand awoke he was lying beside a fire. He groaned and tried to move, but his hands and feet were bound.

"So you're finally awake."

He looked up at the familiar voice. Croftner? Here? Where were the Indians? He shook his head to clear it. He must still be asleep. But a hard boot in his ribs convinced him he wasn't dreaming.

"So we meet again, old friend." Ben stooped and sneered in his face. A lock of white-blond hair fell across his gray eyes. "Did you really think I'd let you get away with taking my girl? But I'm going to do worse to you, Campbell. When I get through with you, you'll wish that bullet had killed you outright."

"How—how did you get me away from the Indians?"

Ben smiled, but the expression was a cruel one. "I paid them to stage an attack. They were just Laramie loafers out for enough money to buy some liquor." He leaned forward and spat in Rand's face. "Are you ready to die, Campbell? You'll pray for death before I'm through with you." His lips twisted.

Rand held his gaze. "You can't frighten me with heaven, Ben."

Ben gaped at him, then stood with an angry oath.

"Don't tell me you've gotten religion," he jeered. "If that doesn't beat all! Hey, Labe, Rand thinks he's going to heaven." He sneered and spat on the ground. "But he's going to find out what hell's really like before we're through."

Rand turned his head as Labe shuffled from behind a rock. Labe's dirty-blond hair fell across his face as he fastened his suspenders. "Sorry to see you're mixed up in this, Labe." Labe's pale-blue eyes widened, but he said nothing.

Ben laughed again, an ugly laugh with no mirth in it. "'Too bad you're mixed up with this, Labe,'" he mimicked. He tossed a shovel toward his younger brother. "Get digging."

Labe cast one agonized glance toward Rand's prone figure, then picked up the shovel and began to dig a small hole. He took a stake out of the knapsack beside the fire and pounded it into the hole, all the while keeping his eyes averted from Rand's gaze.

Rand realized what Ben was planning. He was going to stake him out in the sun. A slow death, but a sure one with no water. The nights would be cold too, even if the days were warm. All he could do was pray he died with dignity.

A few minutes later Labe finished his task and threw the shovel down, then wiped the sweat from his face with his sleeve. "I'm done, Ben." He glanced at Rand, then looked away.

"I'm not blind. Grab his feet." Ben grabbed Rand by his wounded arm, and the men dragged him toward the two posts.

Rand clenched his teeth to keep from crying out from the pain. Beads of sweat broke out on his forehead as he fought to retain consciousness.

Ben knelt and wrapped a strip of rawhide around Rand's left wrist. "Don't just stand there—help me, you fool," he snapped.

Labe shuffled forward and knelt at Rand's feet. Ben grinned as he wound rawhide strips around Rand's other wrist. "Think of me with Sarah as you're lying out here, old friend. Stage two of my plan is being put into action right now. Your little fiancée won't be too thrilled with this part of the plan, but her plan for Sarah was pure genius."

"What are you talking about?" Rand groaned as his wounded arm was wrenched above his head and bound to the stake.

"Your little missy cooked up a pretty good scheme

to help me get Sarah. It's really what gave me the idea for this little rendezvous."

So this was the plan Sarah had heard them talking about. He should have dug into this more. "What about Sarah?"

"You just stew about it while you're dying. But you can go knowing I'll take good care of Sarah."

Labe tied Rand's ankles to the stakes, then stood up, dusting his hands.

"If you leave me here, Labe, you'll never get my blood off your hands," Rand whispered.

"Shut up." Ben kicked him in the side, then turned to his brother. "Get our things and let's get going."

Labe's mouth worked soundlessly, and he hesitated. For an instant Rand thought he was going to defy his brother, but in the end, Labe dropped his head and shuffled off to obey Ben.

The two brothers swung onto their horses and looked down at Rand lying spread-eagled on the rocky ground. "So long, Campbell." Ben's smile was triumphant. "The best man always wins, you know. You were never ruthless enough."

Rand watched as they rode off, biting down on the pleading words struggling to escape. Wouldn't

Croftner love it if he begged for mercy? He turned his head away from the direct glare of the sun and began to pray against whatever they had cooked up for Sarah.

After two days with no water, Rand was delirious. He muttered incoherently, sometimes shouting, sometimes screaming. The nights were bad too. The warm spring days plunged into cold nights and he shuddered with the cold.

At one point he realized he was quoting the twenty-third Psalm. "'Yea, though I walk through the valley of the shadow of death, I will fear no evil.'" He was surprised he still remembered it after all these years. He'd learned it at his grandma's knee when he was eight. But this was the valley of the shadow of death, and somehow, he wasn't afraid to die. Something inside kept him from giving into the fever that racked his body.

The morning of the third day, he awoke relatively clearheaded after a rough night. His lips felt thick and his tongue filled his mouth. Today he would probably die. But at least he could see the land he loved with clear eyes one last time. His eyes closed several times, but he forced them open. This time when he fell asleep, he didn't think he would ever awaken. But the lack of water began to take a heavy toll, and he slipped into delirium for what must be the last time. His final thought was of Sarah, and he prayed for God to watch over her.

FOUR

R and cried out and thrashed as the cooling night woke him, shivering as the chill breeze swept over him. He vaguely remembered a dark face swimming before his eyes off and on. Someone forcing water down his parched throat. He tried to move and found his hands and feet were unbound. He looked to his right and saw that Ranger was tied to a tree nearby.

He sat up slowly, his head spinning. Beside him lay a skin plump with water. He took it and drank greedily, then wiped his mouth. A buffalo robe covered the lower half of his body. Puzzled, he looked around. Who had cut him free? He frowned and tried to concentrate on the dark face at the edge of his memory, but nothing more would come.

Where were Ben and Labe? He looked around slowly as his head continued to clear. The sun lay low in the sky. Only an hour or so of daylight was left. He swallowed another swig of water and shook his head to clear it, then stood. He swayed, then staggered toward his horse.

His mouth watered at the sight of jerky slung over his saddle. He stuffed some into his mouth as he leaned his head against Ranger's flank. Fortified with food and water, he forced himself to swing up into the saddle. He swayed and caught at the pommel to steady himself. He had to make it. Sarah depended on it. He remembered what Ben had said about Jessica, and he had to get back to make sure Sarah was all right. And Jessica. Surely she couldn't be involved with a man like Croftner. Ben had to have said that to upset him.

He urged Ranger to a trot and clung tightly to avoid slipping out of the saddle. Within an hour he was in familiar territory. Maybe he could make Fort

Laramie before it was fully dark. But his horse was exhausted, and he was forced to walk. Rand was still weak from his ordeal, and he had to stop often to catch his breath. He stopped for the night on a bluff about five miles southwest of the fort. Barely conscious, he crawled into his bedroll and closed his eyes.

The weather had warmed to the seventies the last few days. Sarah snatched her bonnet and handed Amelia's to her. "I'm tired of being cooped up. Let's go for a stroll in the sunshine." Amelia followed her into the bright sunshine. Puddles stood in the parade ground, and she stopped to listen to the band practicing.

Her bonnet shaded the glare from her face, and she glanced around. The men should be back from woodcutting detail soon. She noticed Amelia's perusal of her face. "What?"

"You'll have to make a decision about Isaac soon, Sarah. Are you going to marry him if he asks you?"

Sarah pressed her lips together and started off toward the sutler's store. "I don't know. I like him. He's so kind to Joel. And Joel likes him too. That's important to me." She kicked a rock out of her path. "Nothing is as I thought it would be when I came out here. I thought Joel and I would have a home. You and Jacob have been wonderful, but you haven't been able to really settle into married life, not with the two of us living in that tiny space with you both. I should just marry Isaac."

"You don't love him, though."

She cast a sidelong glance at her friend who knew her too well. "Not yet, but I hope to. I can't pine after Rand the rest of my days. He's made his decision very clear."

"I think he regrets his decision."

"I doubt it." Her words died as she saw Jessica waving to them from in front of the store.

"Sarah, Amelia." She was dressed in a cream percale gown lavished with cream lace. Her red hair hung to her shoulders and gleamed in the sunshine. "I was hoping to find you. I haven't seen much of you lately. Isaac has arranged for a detachment to escort Mother and me on a picnic. Would you like to come?"

Sarah glanced at Amelia, who looked as confused as Sarah felt. "Why? You've made no secret of how you feel about me all winter. Why the sudden change of heart?"

Jessica smiled and reached out to touch Sarah's arm. "I realized how petty I was being. You're part of Rand's past, and I'd like us to be friends. Can't we start over? The fort is too small for enmity between us."

Sarah was silent a moment. The jibe about being part of Rand's past stung, but it was true. It was time to let go and heal as many relationships as possible. Besides, she was weary of the tiny area she was allowed. It would be grand to see some new terrain. That was the one thing she hadn't accepted about fort life yet. The restrictions. Back home she was used to going for long rides by herself, wandering in the woods, or just walking along a country road. Now she was not allowed off the fort premises without a guard of at least five soldiers. And it seemed the fort's parade ground got smaller and smaller every day.

Sarah hoped her smile looked genuine. "That sounds lovely. We'll go pack some food."

Jessica patted her arm, then tugged her forward along the wooden walk, Amelia and Mrs. DuBois not far behind. "Don't bother. Mother has packed enough for an entire troop."

Jessica chatted easily as they strolled to the stable. Isaac had their mounts waiting for them, already cinched with sidesaddles. He helped Sarah up, and she smiled into his hazel eyes. Such a kind man. Why couldn't she feel more strongly about him? She'd sensed his impatience at the way she kept him at a distance. She expected a proposal from him at any time.

The women followed the detail of twelve soldiers west toward the purple mountains.

Jessica kept up her smiling chatter, and gradually Sarah relaxed. Was it too much to hope that Jessica might be like this all the time? They found a grassy area near an outcropping of rocks and spread out their blankets away from any melting snowdrifts. The air was pungent with the scent of sage, and the purple mountains in the distance reached up to kiss the blue skies.

After lunch Isaac knelt beside Sarah. "I'd like to bring down some game while we're out here." His soft gaze searched hers, as if trying to determine if she was open to a more serious conversation.

Sarah looked away. "Of course. We'll accompany you."

She gathered up the picnic things, then mounted with the other women. Sarah let her horse pick its way up the winding trail, breathing in the scent of sage.

She reveled in the sense of freedom from the confines of Fort Laramie.

As the men listened with rapt attention to Jessica's story about a ball in Boston, Sarah let her horse walk farther and farther away from them. Even Amelia didn't notice. At the top of the bluff, she slid off her horse and sat where she could look at the fort below her. She chuckled at Isaac's sudden agitation when he discovered she was missing.

She raised a hand and opened her mouth to call to him when her horse whinnied behind her. She stood quickly and turned to see an Indian warrior, heavily painted, galloping toward her. She froze in terror, then tried to put her foot into the stirrup to mount.

But the Indian was upon her in an instant. He leaned down and scooped her up, his horse barely pausing as he caught her.

Sarah struggled to get away, gagging at the odor of bear grease and sweat, but his arm was like a steel band around her waist. She screamed, certain she was doomed. But the crack of a rifle sounded and the Indian slumped against her, his arm loosening.

She wrenched free and fell from the horse. Stunned from the swiftness of both the attack and her rescue, she lay on the hard ground as the Indian wheeled away, his face glazed with pain, holding a hand to his bloody shoulder.

Rooster galloped out of a stand of trees, his cavalry cap gone and spiky red hair standing on end. "What's wrong with you, gal? Don't you got no sense atall?" He slid off his horse and pulled her to her feet. "Git on that horse now!" He shoved her up into the saddle. "There's prob'ly more of them sneakin' varmints around. We gotta git to the fort." He slapped her horse's rump, and they started down the bluff.

Isaac, Mrs. DuBois, and Amelia, with the rest of the soldiers, met them at the bottom. Isaac's face was tight with anger. But before he could say anything, they heard a whoop behind them and turned to see a group of Indians charging toward them.

"Get going!" Isaac fell back and fired at the Indians to give Rooster time to get the girls to the safety of the fort.

Amelia and Sarah kicked their horses into a mad dash for the fort as Mrs. DuBois screamed and moved faster than Sarah had ever seen. Jessica kicked her horse into a gallop, her face calm, and the rest of the soldiers brought up the rear.

A bullet whistled by Sarah's head as she clung to the horse's back. Then her horse stumbled and she catapulted into a thorny bush. Her skin was pierced in a dozen places, and she lay there too stunned to even move.

A young warrior galloped up, brandishing a knife. Before she could even think to scream, he cut her loose from the thornbush and hauled her up in front of him.

Sarah tried to struggle away, but her head was throbbing from the fall and soon darkness descended.

The next morning Rand awoke ravenous. His sunburn still throbbed, but he was stable. His store of food was all gone, and his ammunition was low, so he took his rifle and made his way down to the river. It wasn't long before he shot a jackrabbit. It was tough and stringy as he ate it hot from the spit, but it would do. At least it would give him the strength he needed to get back.

He saddled up Ranger and swung up into the saddle. In spite of the deceptive distances, he knew he'd be home soon. The fort drew nearer very quickly.

Now he could make out the individual buildings. There was the commissary and the stable. The barracks and the hospital. Was he too late to help Sarah? He urged Ranger into a gallop.

He arrived about eight o'clock. There seemed to be an uncommon amount of activity as dozens of soldiers jostled one another in their hurry to catch a mount and saddle up. Rooster, his voice shrill with emotion, called for a fresh horse.

His heart pounding, Rand spotted Jacob and Isaac saddling horses beside the post headquarters. He kicked his mount into a canter and pulled up beside them. "What's going on?"

Jacob's voice was grim. "Indians got Sarah."

The clipped words hit Rand like a blow. He felt light-headed with shock. "When?" He'd been worried about Ben and Jessica's plan, and he should have been praying for safety from the Sioux.

"This morning. We're just back for fresh horses and supplies. You coming?"

"Let me get a fresh mount." Outwardly he was calm, but inwardly a cauldron of emotion was churning. Anger, guilt, love. He realized in a blinding instant what a fool he'd been. He'd never be able to ignore his feelings for her. He and Sarah had something precious, and he had treated it as something of inconsequence. And now it might be too late. He shuddered at the thought of what Sarah had perhaps already endured. He followed Isaac and Jacob out of the fort as they caught up with Rooster on his way to pick up the trail.

Just before dusk they found a spot where a large group of horses had trampled the ground. Rand knelt in the dust. "Some of these prints belong to white men. Look here, Isaac. Shod hoof prints and boot heels."

Isaac knelt beside him and touched the prints. "Looks like two, maybe three, men."

Rooster came up behind them. "Sure am glad to see you, boy. You look bad, though. Yer skin's blistered and peeling. What happened to you? How'd you git away from them Injuns?"

"I'll tell you later." Finding Sarah was more important.

Rooster nodded and knelt beside them. "What'd ya find, boys?"

Rand gestured to the boot prints. "What do you make of this, Rooster? What would white men be doing with a pack of Sioux?"

Rooster studied the ground for a moment. "Don't

look too good, young fellers. Don't look too good at all." He stood and scratched his red hair. "Injuns and white men. Renegades, most likely." His brown eyes were compassionate as he turned to Rand. "Looks like maybe they got Sarah."

Rand shuddered. He felt as though his whole body had suddenly turned to ice. Renegade white men were the worst scum to walk the earth. They lived with the Sioux and used them for their own purposes.

Jacob clapped a hand on his brother's shoulder. "Don't give up hope yet, Rand. We'll find her. White men move slower than Indians. We have a better chance of catching them now."

Rand nodded, but he knew Sarah was lost to him. He felt almost crazy with worry and grief as Rooster found the trail, and the detachment followed it up into the Laramie Mountains. The landscape grew more barren as loose rock over a bed of sand made travel more and more treacherous. As they rode, Rand told Rooster and Jacob about his ordeal and what Ben had said.

Jacob ducked under a low-hanging tree. "What if this is part of Ben's plan? Maybe he hired renegades to grab her."

Rand shook his head. "Even Ben wouldn't stoop to working with men like that."

By the time it was too dark to follow the trail any longer, they were near the peak of the mountain. The night air was already cold, and a crisp tang to the air mingled with the scent of sage and the smoke from the fire as Rand unloaded his supplies and prepared to bed down near Jacob and Isaac.

Rooster took his rifle out of its scabbard on his saddle. "I'll take the first watch." He walked over to a large boulder.

Rand lay on the hard ground and stared up at the sky, vaguely aware of the crackling fire to his right as he gazed at the bright panorama of stars. The fire pushed back the blackness of the night, but nothing could push away the blackness in his soul.

The plaintive howl of a pack of coyotes somewhere in the valley below him somehow added to his anguish. He prayed fervently for Sarah's safety, but he was so consumed with worry, he couldn't keep his thoughts together. The fire died to embers before he finally slept.

FIVE

When Sarah awoke she found herself on a pallet on a hard, dirt-packed floor. She sat up slowly and looked around the tiny one-room cabin. A rank odor rose from the grimy blanket over her, and she pushed it off with a shudder of disgust as she rose to get a better view of her surroundings.

Her head throbbed and the room spun as she took a step toward the small, oilskin-covered windows. She paused until her head cleared, then moved gingerly toward the door. She raised the latch and tugged at the door, but it refused to budge no matter how hard she pulled. She leaned her throbbing head against it and tried to think.

Those savages would be back any minute. What was she going to do? She could still see the painted face of the Indian who grabbed her. But why wasn't she at an Indian camp? And whose old cabin was this anyway?

But there were no answers to her questions, so she pushed away the fears and looked around for another avenue of escape. Her body ached in a hundred places from her contact with the thornbush, and she limped as she picked through the debris on the dirt floor.

She found a small stool among the litter of papers, old tin cans, and rags and dragged it under the window. Standing on the stool, she pulled the torn oilcloth away from the window and tried to pull herself through.

But the tiny opening was much too small for even Sarah's slim shoulders, and the stool collapsed under her weight, one leg rolling useless across the floor, as she fell to the ground. She was hungry and thirsty and scared. Judging by the light, it was close to noon, so she must have been unconscious nearly twenty-four hours. No wonder her mouth was like cotton.

She sat there until the sun no longer shone through

the east window, feeling more and more abandoned. What if she was left here to die with no food or water? Panic overwhelmed her, and she ran to the door and pounded on it. She backed away when she heard horses approaching. The click of a lock being pulled back on the door.

Trembling, she faced the door, so frightened she felt faint. If only she could see who was on the other side. Had the savages come back, or was she about to be rescued? She didn't dare hope.

The sudden flood of sunlight into the dark cabin blinded her momentarily, then she blinked in surprise as she recognized the two figures framed in the doorway.

"Be-Ben?" she croaked through her parched throat. "Thank the Lord you're here."

Although she would rather anyone else rescue her, Ben was a welcome surprise from the savages she'd expected. She had opened her mouth to thank him when she noticed how unsurprised he seemed to see her.

"Been awake long? I wanted to give you time to appreciate my appearance."

"You knew . . . I was here?" Her chest thumped hard, and she took a step back.

"Of course." He kicked some refuse away from

the door. "Shut the door, Labe." He reached out and touched a lock of her hair, and she flinched away. His lips tightened as he dropped his hand. "The Indians were eager for the guns I offered for the 'soldier girl with hair like the sun.' But I must give credit where credit's due. Jessica came up with the idea."

Sarah felt the blood drain from her face. Ben and Jessica had arranged for her kidnapping? But why? Her lips quivered as she forced back tears of weakness. She didn't want to give him the satisfaction of seeing her cry.

"Aren't you interested in why you're here?" The cruel light in Ben's eyes grew as she took a step back. "Remember that marriage we were supposed to have? You should have been my wife by now, and I aim to put that to rights." He pulled her to him and wrapped a hand in her hair.

Pain encased her head as he tightened his grip on her. "Let go of me." She couldn't hold back a moan when he pulled even harder.

"Too bad about your beloved Rand," he sneered. "You have no one to blame for his death but yourself."

A shudder shook Sarah's frame, and she closed her eyes. "Wha–what do you mean?"

"I'm sure he's dead by now." He smirked. "Being staked out in the sun without food or water isn't a pleasant way to die, but he deserved every bit of torment."

Rand dead? She *wouldn't* believe it. "You're lying," she whispered. After all, she'd believed Ben before— and look what had happened.

"Think so? Tell her, Labe."

His brother looked away and shuffled his feet. She stared into Ben's face. How had she ever considered marrying him? The silence grew heavy as Ben stared back at her with an unsettling conviction in his eyes. He'd fooled her before, though. Labe's nervous shuffle broke the silence.

Sarah turned her eyes toward him. "Please. Please, Labe. Help me."

Labe's eyes darted from his brother's set face to Sarah's. "Come on, Ben. Let's take her back. She won't say nothin', will you, Sarah?"

"No. No, of course not." She wet her dry lips with the tip of her tongue. "Just take me back to the fort, and I'll say you rescued me from the Indians. You'll be heroes."

Ben's lip curled. "You must take me for a fool!" He let go of Sarah's hair and shoved her off her feet, then spun toward Labe. "Get out!" He pushed his brother out of the door, then shut and locked it.

While Ben's back was turned, her hand groped along the dirty floor. Her seeking fingers closed around the broken stool leg. Ben turned back toward her and leaned down with a smile. She twisted around and with one last desperate effort, she smashed the stool leg against his head. He slumped against her without a sound.

She scrambled to her feet, rushed to the door, and pulled it open. She blinked as she surveyed her surroundings. The tiny cabin was in a small clearing enclosed by heavy forest. A meadow filled with wild-flowers was in front of the door, and a narrow, barely discernible path ran through the middle of the meadow. She caught a glimpse of Labe's head over near a stand of aspen with his back to the cabin.

Watching to make sure Labe didn't see her, she stumbled along the path, casting furtive glances behind her to make sure neither Labe nor Ben was following her. The path narrowed further, then disappeared at the bank of a small stream. Sarah sank to her knees and drank.

Birds twittered from the budding branches above

her head, but that was the only sound as she followed the stream into the forest. The stream soon joined a larger river, and Sarah rushed along the bank. How long would it be before Ben regained consciousness? He would pursue her. She had to get as far away as she could.

Labe had fallen asleep leaning against an aspen tree, but he woke with a jump when Ben staggered out of the cabin.

"Where is she?" Ben looked around wildly.

"Who?" Labe peered past Ben into the dark cabin as if trying to see Sarah.

"Who do you think?" Ben held his aching head and tried to think. "Why didn't you stop her?"

"Honest, Ben, I didn't see nothin'." He backed away from his brother and stared slack jawed as Ben stumbled toward the horses. "Where you going? I thought we was going to hole up here for a few days."

"Plans have changed." Ben tightened the cinch on his mare's belly. "Thanks to you, I've got to track Miss Sarah down."

"Can't we just leave her be?"

Ben wiped away a bit of blood from his face. "She's not getting off after what she did to me." He swung into the saddle and waited impatiently while Labe followed suit. Ben's face burned. No one got in Ben Croftner's way without paying for it.

The sun told her it was midafternoon, and Sarah stopped beside the river. Her head was light from lack of food, and she had to rest for a moment. She sank down on a large rock and looked around, trying to think. She had to find something to eat or she'd never make it.

Wearily, she forced herself to her feet again and searched the bushes, grateful for the forest lore Rand had taught her when they were growing up. After several minutes, she found some berries she knew were edible, and she crammed handfuls into her mouth, grimacing at their bitter taste. Using her fingernails, she dug the roots of another edible plant out of the ground. She washed the soil off in the river and then crunched them down.

A little clearer-headed, she stared along the river-bank again. She would make it. She strode off with new determination.

But by the next morning, she was no longer so certain. She itched from what seemed like a thousand mosquito bites. The insects had swarmed around her all night, a living haze of biting misery. So weak now from hunger and fatigue, she could barely stagger with one foot in front of the other. She'd startled awake with every sound all night. Coyotes had howled, their voices closer than she had ever heard them, and once a large animal had snuffled right next to her, causing her to freeze, too terrified to move for several long minutes.

Now, as the sun tipped to the west, her steps slowed. She rounded a curve in the river, forcing herself for-ward, and then stood still.

She was face-to-face with a band of ten or so Sioux warriors. Their faces were painted and one young man had a livid scar across his cheek. The blood drained from her face, and then darkness claimed her.

SIX

Rand rode silently through the woods, hardly looking at the other men for fear he'd see the fear he felt in their eyes. Jacob reined his horse in suddenly and dismounted. He bent over and picked something off the ground.

"What is it?" Rand's voice was hoarse. He held out his hand and Jacob dropped a brooch into it.

They'd both seen it many times. The delicate filigree rose customarily adorned the bodice of Sarah's dress. Rand had given it to her for her sixteenth birthday before he left for the war. Hard to believe it had been over three years.

He stared at the dainty pin, and his face turned hard as he fought to control the pain that surged through him. "At least we know we're on the right trail. Everyone always said Rooster could follow a wood tick on solid rock." Rand picked up the reins, gripped by a renewed sense of urgency. "Let's get going."

Rooster led the way, his keen eyes following the fresh trail. They splashed across the stream and picked their way up a steep hill. He glanced around at the silent men as they paused at the top. "Reckon we all fell a little bit in love with that gal." His voice was hoarse.

"Don't say it like she's gone!" Isaac's knuckles were white where they gripped the reins. "We can't be more than a few hours behind her." He urged his horse forward and took the lead through a line of trees.

Rand and Jacob, following close behind, reined in at the sound of a startled snort. Two bear cubs bleated and rolled toward their mother. Mama bear swung around from her perusal of a fallen tree trunk, ready to face the threat to her offspring.

Rand's eyes met the grizzly's. She roared angrily

as she rose to her hind feet, a good seven feet tall. Her mouth wide with another roar, she dropped to all fours and charged toward them.

Jacob was closest, and his horse shied. He fell to the ground. The bear loomed over him and opened her giant mouth. He grabbed for his gun, but it lay three feet away where it had fallen from his holster when he was catapulted from the saddle. He scrabbled backward, away from the grizzly.

"Lie still, boy!" Rooster aimed his Winchester at the bear's head, just as Rand frantically aimed his own gun.

The rifles barked, but not before the grizzly swiped at Jacob's leg with her claws. She swung her head in dull surprise, then crashed to the ground beside Jacob.

Blood was already pouring from Jacob's leg, soaking his torn pants. "Quick, hand me the canteen!" Rand fell to his knees beside his brother.

Rooster handed him the canteen. "Clean it good, boy, or it'll fester for sure. No telling where that bear's claws have been."

Rand ripped the fabric away from the wound and splashed it with water again and again. Jacob's flesh was flayed so badly that the bone gleamed through the shredded skin. Rand tried to keep the dismay from his face as he bound the wound with a clean handkerchief.

Jacob's face was pale and sweat sheened his forehead as he gritted his teeth against the pain. "Sorry, Rand." His face contracted frustration. "We were so close."

Rand patted his brother's leg. "You're going to be all right." He prayed the words were true. But he couldn't abandon Sarah. Somehow he had to arrange to get Jacob back to the fort while he pressed on to find her.

Isaac crouched beside him and gave Jacob a sip of water. "How bad is it?"

Rand turned his head away so Jacob couldn't hear. "Bad. It's deep in his thigh muscle—to the bone. He'll be in even more pain when the shock wears off. We need to find someplace for him to hole up." He paused bleakly. "He won't be riding for a while."

Isaac nodded. "I hunted this area last year. If I remember right, there's a small cabin just beyond the woods to our north. Let's make for there. It's almost dark anyway."

Rand fought to keep despair from settling in as they made a rough travois to carry Jacob. This delay could be deadly for Sarah.

Isaac led the way through the trees. Rand spared a thought for the motherless bear cubs, but there was nothing they could do for them. He found himself smiling, thinking that if Sarah were there, she would probably have insisted they catch the cubs and bring them home to raise. His smile faded to a frown of pain as he was washed anew with fear for Sarah.

The light was murky by the time they stepped out of the forest and into a small meadow clearing. The cabin squatted against the sloping north side, and they hurried toward its meager haven.

The open door creaked in the gentle breeze as they swung off their horses. "Me and the men will take care of the horses," Rooster said. "Git that boy inside. Better clean the wound again too."

Rand and Isaac carefully lifted Jacob off the travois and carried him into the dark cabin. They laid him on a moldy mattress in the corner.

"Light a lantern, Isaac." Rand eased his brother's boots off and untied the handkerchief on Jacob's leg.

Isaac lit the lantern, and the dim glow pushed the shadows back. The wound had reopened from the jostling on the travois, and Jacob lay unconscious.

One of the other men came in with a small flask in

his hand. "Rooster says he brought it along for medicinal purposes."

Rand uncapped the flask and poured a generous amount of alcohol into Jacob's gaping wound. He thrashed and cried out, then lapsed back into unconsciousness as Rand rebound the wound.

"I reckon that's all we can do," he said to Isaac.

"Except pray."

Rand looked at Isaac, then back at his brother. He nodded and knelt on the floor, Isaac beside him as they each asked God for his help. After a few minutes, Isaac got to his feet, but Rand stayed where he was. At last he stood, and a new peace filled his heart. He felt his first real sense of hope that they might find Sarah alive and well.

They made up their beds on the dirt floor. Rand checked on Jacob several times throughout the night as his brother thrashed restlessly. Finally at dawn, he touched Jacob's forehead and found it cool. He breathed a sigh as he pulled on his boots and woke the others.

The first rays of sunrise pushed through bare branches as Rand sat eating a cold breakfast of hardtack and dried meat under a tree. They had to find her today.

Rooster burst into the clearing. "She was here! Our little gal was here!"

Rand jumped up and gripped Rooster's arm. "What are you talking about?"

"Our Sarah was here. Look!" Rooster held out a scrap of familiar green-and-yellow calico.

Rand fingered the soft cloth. "Where did you find it?" He pressed it against his lips and inhaled, but there was no lingering fragrance other than of mud.

"Down by the stream. And I found her trail—she's alone." Rooster almost danced in jubilation.

Rand stared at the scrap of fabric, almost giddy with relief. She'd gotten away from whoever had held her captive. "Let's check Jacob."

When he stepped into the cabin, he found Jacob sitting up, sipping a thin gruel made of water and hardtack. He gave them a wan smile. "Sorry, Rand. Guess I won't be in any shape to travel for a few days."

Rand nodded. "I'm just thankful you're alive." He grinned, eager to wipe the look of guilt off Jacob's face. "I have to wonder, though, if you didn't get in that bear's way just so you'd have a good story to tell back at Bedlam."

He waited until Jacob smiled weakly, and then Rand turned to the group of privates who were crouching against the wall eating their hardtack. "I want you soldiers to stay with Jacob until he can travel, then get him back to the fort. Isaac and Rooster will come with me to find Sarah." He cocked an eyebrow at his two friends. "Okay with you?"

"Let's get going." Isaac's eyes were hooded.

Rand eyed him. He hadn't even stopped to think how this was affecting Isaac. Their affection for the same woman wasn't something either of them would be comfortable talking about either.

Rooster nodded. "I'll saddle up the horses."

Fifteen minutes later, Rand was almost jubilant as they followed Sarah's clear trail.

"That gal will never make an Injun," Rooster muttered. "She leaves a path even a greenhorn could follow."

Near noon, they rounded a bend in the river they were following and Rooster stopped short. He whistled in dismay. Sarah's clear tracks were obliterated by unshod pony tracks and moccasin prints. "Looks like the Injuns caught her."

Rand stood staring at the telltale marks, his heart pounding. So close to finding her and now this. He swallowed hard as he fought to hold on to his new faith and hope. "Can you tell what kind of Indians?"

"Hard to say, but I'd guess Sioux."

They followed the trail for the rest of the afternoon. Rand struggled to pray, but despair kept rearing its head.

One of the Sioux warriors gave Sarah jerky and fresh water before jabbering and pulling her to her feet. In spite of her terror, she was grateful for the food. She'd never been so hungry in her life. The jerky was tough, but she didn't know when anything had tasted so good.

She turned and looked back at the way they'd come. If Rand lived, he would find her. She was sure of it.

The young warrior with the scar on his face pulled her up behind him on his pony, and she wrinkled her nose at the stench of sweat and bear grease. The Sioux band picked its way along a faint trail through the forest. Sarah would never have recognized it was a trail, but once they had followed it for a while, she was able to see the slight impression from other Indian ponies. Twilight was sending out long, golden shadows by the time they turned the crest of a hill. Campfires and teepee shapes became visible below them in the valley beside a stream.

Children jabbered and women stared at her with hostile eyes as the warriors paraded through the camp, raising their bows and spears in triumphant shrieks. Sarah fought unconsciousness as she tried not to droop wearily against the young warrior's back. Her vision blurred and doubled as he stopped beside a teepee and slid to the ground.

He pulled her down, and she fought his grip on her arms. "Let go of me."

He grunted, then thrust her inside the teepee and closed the flap, encasing her in darkness. She was too weary to do more than stumble to a soft pile of furs and sink into instant sleep.

When Sarah awoke she was in a dark, cool place. Strange chanting filled her head, and she heard the rumbles of unfamiliar voices. But the words were all jumbled together, and nothing made any sense. She tried to rise and was surprised to find she could move her hands and feet. She had thought the Indians would tie her up so she couldn't escape in the night. The sounds outside were distant and not threatening, so she snuggled back down in the furs and fell asleep again.

The next time she awoke, she was not alone. A beautiful Indian girl knelt beside her and offered her a bowl of stew that smelled wonderful. She took it and ate eagerly. It was flavored with unfamiliar herbs, but the meat and vegetables were tasty. The young woman smiled, then quickly stepped outside and closed the flap on the teepee behind her.

Sarah's shoulder protested as she got to her feet. Swaying weakly, she started toward the flap, then staggered and sank back to the ground. She was just too tired to push herself any longer. She returned to the bearskin rug and stared at the opening to the teepee. What if Rand was really dead like Ben said? She pushed the thought away. He couldn't be dead. And he would find her.

She looked around curiously. She'd always wondered

what a teepee looked like inside, but she'd never been in one. Not even Morning Song's.

The teepee was large, at least ten feet in diameter. In the center was a tripod arrangement that supported a pot over what were now cold ashes, although a pile of buffalo chips lay heaped to the side. Spears and knives hung from the lodge poles, and buffalo robes were piled to one side. Pelts of various animals—dove, wolverine, raccoon, and antelope—were in various stages of tanning on a rack of some kind.

She dragged her gaze away from the lodge furnishings as the flap opened and the Indian warrior came in. A fierce scowl creased his young face, and Sarah's heart pounded in trepidation. It was the youth with the terrible scar on his cheek she'd seen before.

"He–hello," she stammered. Then she smiled as she remembered the Sioux greeting Isaac had taught her. *"Wash ta cola."*

He merely grunted, his black eyes roaming over Sarah's tangled hair. He reached out and touched a bright red-gold lock.

She forced herself not to flinch. "Sarah." She gestured at herself. "My name is Sarah."

The warrior nodded, a smile winking across his face so quickly Sarah thought she'd imagined it.

The flap lifted again as the young Sioux maiden entered. She reminded Sarah of a young antelope, all long limbs yet curiously graceful. Sarah's heart clenched as she thought of Morning Song.

"You awake," she said, her dark eyes liquid with a hidden smile.

"You speak English." Sarah smiled in relief.

"Little. Little English. Live at mission one year." The girl squatted and offered her another bowl of stew. "You eat."

Sarah wasn't really hungry any longer, but since she intended to escape at the first opportunity, she needed to build up her strength as quickly as possible.

The boy grunted again and said something to the girl. "Little Wolverine say you belong to blue coat with eyes like eagle. Soldier not kill Little Wolverine in battle. Why?"

Sarah searched her memory, but she couldn't remember Rand mentioning an incident like he described. "I don't know," she admitted reluctantly.

The girl translated to the young man and he fired a volley of words back at her. "He say blue coat with eagle eyes spare Little Wolverine. Little Wolverine save you." She pretended to weigh her hands until they were on an equal level.

"Yes. Even. Thank you." Sarah looked into the dark eyes beside her and thanked God for sending such an unlikely rescuer. They weren't going to hurt her.

SEVEN

S arah's strength grew daily on the good food White Dove brought. She gave Sarah a beautifully beaded Indian dress to replace her torn dress and braided her hair.

Sarah and the young maiden grew to be friends—she felt an almost uncanny sense of friendship and identification with her, as if she'd known her all her life—and by the third day Sarah felt at home in the busy Sioux camp. The children were curious about her and soon lost their shyness when she appeared.

White Dove was happy to translate their innumerable questions.

But Sarah grew more anxious daily. Where was Rand? Was there any truth to what Ben told her? Could Rand really be dead—or did he think she was dead? And Joel would be frantic. What would become of her little brother if Sarah never returned? She couldn't bear to think of him with Wade. Maybe Amelia and Jacob would raise him.

"Why you so sad?" White Dove asked as they fished in the stream just after dawn on the fourth day.

Sarah clambered out of the water and sat on a large rock, White Dove following close behind her. "I miss my friends and my little brother. You know the word *brother*?"

White Dove nodded. "I have small brother." She held out her hand to her waist.

"And I worry about the bad man who tried to hurt me. He may be looking for me still."

White Dove nodded slowly, her dark eyes compassionate. "Little Wolverine take you back soon. Then debt to blue coat is paid. And Little Wolverine say Sarah cry no more. He know man who hurt Sarah. He make sure he not hurt Sarah again." She reached over and touched Sarah's arm shyly. "White Dove miss Sarah."

"I'll miss you too," she said hoarsely. "Thank Little Wolverine for me. You are both good friends."

Just a few days with the Sioux had shown her how alike they all were. Little Wolverine and the other Indians had no idea how many settlers were clamoring to take away the Indian hunting grounds. And Rand might actually have to fight Little Wolverine some day. She couldn't stand the thought of the bright young warrior lying dead on a field of battle.

She picked up her string of fish and followed White Dove back to camp. Why was life never simple?

Rand and his companions followed the trail as it led through rocky hills and sagebrush-choked gullies. When they ran low on rations, Rand and Isaac brought down an antelope and cut it into strips for jerky, smoking it overnight over a low fire. Rand alternated between worry for Sarah and concern for Jacob back at the cabin.

Four days from the fort, they awoke to a leaden

sky with a stiff, moisture-laden breeze whipping across the stark landscape. If it rained, the trail would be washed away. And they were so close. They hurriedly saddled up and rode out.

But their haste was useless. The storm struck with its usual force in the mountains. Hail rained down on them, and they were forced to take shelter under an overhang in the gully. Thunder boomed around them as torrents of rain fell and lightning crackled overhead.

"We've got to git to high ground!" Rooster shouted above the crashing thunder. "This here's a real gully washer. There's liable to be a flash flood any time."

Staying as close to the rock wall as possible, they led their horses up the rocky hill. Halfway up the side of the slope, Rand looked down. A mountain of water swept away the tangle of sagebrush and aspen where they'd been only minutes before.

"This here's prob'ly high enough." Rooster paused under an overhang.

They crouched there, hugging the cold side of the rocky wall. The horses shifted restlessly, but the men managed to hang on to the reins. Finally the downpour was over. Steamy mist shimmered in the heat as the sun broke through the clouds, and they emerged from their sanctuary.

Rand gaped at the changed landscape. The flash flood had carved new gullies and filled in old low spots as the raging water carried away everything in its path. He stood surveying the damage as dismay swept over him. The trail to Sarah would never have survived such rain.

"Don't take on so, boy. We ain't done by a long shot."

"What do you mean, Rooster? How will we ever find her now?"

"I've scouted these parts before. Over yonder peak is one of the Injuns' favorite camping grounds. We'll just mosey on over there, and maybe we'll find our little gal."

Galvanized, Rand leaped astride his horse as Rooster led the way and Isaac brought up the rear. By nightfall they were in a line of trees overlooking an Indian campground. The teepees glowed with color from the sunset. They caught glimpses of dimly illuminated figures moving around the campfires.

"Now what?" Rand asked.

"Now we stay put till they're sleepin'." The old Indian fighter took off his hat and smoothed his red hair. "Then we sneak in and look around for our Miss Sarah."

They tied their horses to a tree and hunkered down to wait. Rand kept watch while the other two tried to catch a little sleep. He was just about to wake Isaac for his turn at watch when he noticed a movement just below their lookout. He cocked his rifle and the other two were awake in an instant.

"What is it?" Isaac whispered.

"Don't know. Thought I saw something." Rand searched the spot again, but he froze when he heard a sound on the slope above them. He swiveled his head and faced a row of fiercely painted Indians holding spears, all pointed at him and his friends.

They were obviously outnumbered, so when one of the Indians motioned for them to drop their guns, they obeyed. The Sioux bound their hands with brutal efficiency, then marched them down the slope to the camp. They thrust them roughly into a large teepee and fastened the flap firmly behind them.

Rand could see the outline of a guard through the buckskin. Some rescuers they were. Now they were all in the same uncomfortable spot with Sarah, if she was even here.

Rand squatted on a buffalo robe. "Why didn't they kill us outright?"

"They're probably saving us for some special ceremony," Isaac said, sitting down on a buffalo robe. "We'd best get some sleep. They'll be on their guard tonight, but maybe tomorrow we can find a way to escape."

Rand sat up just before dawn, too keyed up to lay down any longer. He listened to the sounds of the camp beginning to stir around him. He understood none of the guttural language outside as women lit fires and called to one another.

Diffused light gradually lifted the darkness inside their teepee as the bustle outside increased. Finally the flap lifted, and a young man stepped through, followed by an Indian girl. Rand immediately recognized him as the warrior he had spared in the battle the week before. And he was the one whose face he'd seen in his delirium.

Rooster recognized the boy too. "I told you you'd be sorry."

But Rand felt no fear as he looked into the youth's calm, dark eyes.

The girl stepped forward and smiled at him. "Do

not fear. Little Wolverine your friend. But he ask, 'Why you not shoot him?'"

Rand hesitated. His reasons would probably sound silly, but there was no help for it. "Little Wolverine reminded me of my younger brother. You know the word *brother*?"

The girl nodded. "One who shares mother and father?"

Rand nodded. "I have a younger brother about the same age as Little Wolverine. I saw that same brave spirit in Little Wolverine."

The girl smiled as she translated. The youth's black eyes never left Rand's face as she explained. Then he nodded and barked an order to the girl. She gave Rand a slight smile, then slipped out of the teepee. Moments later Sarah stepped through the flap behind the Indian girl.

"Sarah!"

Her green eyes widened and she gasped as Rand started toward her. "Rand?" She ran into his open arms.

Sarah burrowed her face in the rough fabric of Rand's shirt. His strong arms encased her, and she never wanted to leave this embrace she'd thought she'd never feel again. "How did you find me?"

"Rooster." He touched the bruise on her cheek, then frowned when she flinched. "Who did this to you? And how'd you get away from the renegades who had you?"

Just past him, she saw Isaac staring at the two of them. What was he thinking? She pushed away from Rand. "I–I came to a cabin." He wouldn't understand. Last time Ben had tried to force her to marry him, Rand jumped to the wrong conclusion. "Later," she whispered. She turned to the two Sioux standing silent behind her. "I would have died if it weren't for my friends. I'd like you to meet Little Wolverine and White Dove."

Rand held out his hand to the two Sioux. "I don't know what to say—how to thank you."

The girl smiled. "Sarah is friend. We miss her. You leave in morning for soldier fort but first we have feast."

Rooster and Isaac crowded close and hugged Sarah. Isaac's hug was brief, and he quickly stepped back. She hated to see the hurt in his eyes. "Thanks for saving me."

"I'm glad you're all right." He moved to the side of the teepee and folded muscular arms over his chest.

Rooster grabbed her in a bear hug. "No how were we going home without you."

She hugged him back, unashamed of the tears of joy that trickled down her cheeks. "Thank you, Rooster. They couldn't have found me without you."

She wanted to get Rand alone, to find out what Ben had tried to do to him. And how did she tell him about Jessica's role in her capture? Was it even true?

White Dove motioned to Rand. "Your wound. I will heal."

He sat down and let her smear an ointment on his wound. The stench made Sarah wrinkle her nose, but Rand endured the young woman's ministrations.

Sarah glanced at Isaac, who continued to stare at her as if he was trying to puzzle out something. This ordeal had shown her how deep her feelings for Rand still ran. How could she marry someone else when she knew she'd never get over Rand?

She joined Isaac by the teepee opening. "You have questions. I can see them in your eyes."

"I think the answers are clear. I'd hoped you'd find me a suitable substitute for Rand, but I can see that is never going to happen."

She looked down at the dirt floor. "I don't think so either. I like you, Isaac, so much. I'm sorry."

"Don't be. Better to find out now. I think he knows his own heart now too."

Her pulse throbbed in her neck, but an ache settled over her heart. "I wish that were true, but even if he realized he still loves me, he's a man of honor. He won't go back on his word to Jessica."

Reeking of something that smelled like rotting flesh, Rand joined them. "Sounds like a lot of commotion outside."

Sarah heard it then, the noise of horses and voices. She motioned to White Dove and Little Wolverine. "What's going on?"

The two Sioux walked nearer. White Dove glanced at Sarah, then back to Rand. "We go to make war with Red Cloud at Powder River."

Rand shook his head and looked hard at the young warrior. "Don't go, Little Wolverine. I don't want anything to happen to you. Tell him not to go," he appealed to White Dove.

The boy drew himself up straight and taut as White Dove translated. "He say, 'Should Little Wolverine stay in camp like dog and let others fight for his family? Soon people have no hunting grounds. Whites take all. Red Cloud say Indians must fight or be forced to farm.'"

The boy spat in the dust. "He say, 'Lakota not dirt diggers.'" Little Wolverine's face softened as he spoke again and White Dove continued to translate. "But he say, 'Rand and Little Wolverine brothers. They not fight.'"

"No, my brother." Rand laid a hand on Little Wolverine's shoulder. "We'll not fight. And someday I hope we meet again."

The boy clasped his hand over Rand's large, square hand as though he understood his words before White Dove translated them. His dark eyes were warm with friendship.

Sarah's heart squeezed at the thought of the hardships coming to her new friends. There was nothing she could do either. Nothing any of them could do. The fight for western lands would not be over anytime soon.

EIGHT

Amelia watched the hills surrounding the fort every day, anxious for word of Sarah. The main detachment had returned, hauling Jacob home two days ago, but no one had heard a word from the three who pushed on after Sarah. Her husband paced their small quarters as he waited for word of his brother. When she'd first seen his wound, she'd shuddered, but Jacob was recovering much better than she'd feared.

After breakfast on the third day of Jacob's return, Amelia sat on the porch, watching as the cavalry prepared for maneuvers. Joel sat listlessly beside her, and she put her hand on his arm. "Hang on to your hope, Joel. Maybe Jacob will have news when he gets back."

Tears hung on his lashes. "He has to find her. He has to!"

She touched his cheek. "He will."

"Boots and saddles." Captain Brown shouted the familiar command to mount, and the cavalry swung up onto their horses and rode out of the fort.

Jacob limped across the parade ground to join her and Joel. "The commander says there is still no word. They haven't shown up at Fort Caspar or the Platte River Bridge Station."

Amelia burst into tears and jumped up to bury her face against Jacob's chest. "I have a terrible feeling she's dead. And we'll never know for sure."

Jacob held her close, and she tried to take comfort from his strength. She had a dreadful feeling she'd never see any of them again.

Joel stood suddenly and pointed west. "What's that?"

Jacob turned and looked, then grew still, his gaze scanning the slope to the west of the fort. He pulled Amelia away. "Wait here."

"What is it?"

She shaded her eyes with her hand and saw four riders coming down the rocky incline toward the fort. And one of them, dressed in buckskin like an Indian maiden, had sunny red-gold hair. With a sob of relief, she picked up her skirts and ran after Jacob.

"They've got her!" a sentry to the west of the fort shouted as soldiers ran from the mess hall and barracks to greet their beloved Sarah. Amelia wasn't the only one who had just about given up hope.

Soldiers lined the road and cheered as the four travelers, tired and dusty, rode into the fort.

"Sarah!"

With a sob of joy, Sarah slipped off her mare and fell into Amelia's arms. Laughing and crying, she hugged Amelia, then Joel as soldiers cheered and whistled and slapped each other on the backs. Even the post commander was out to greet them.

Amelia looked up at Rand. "I knew you'd find her."

He grinned down at her. "Always. I'll never let her go."

Amelia caught her breath. Did he mean what she thought he meant?

Joel clung to Sarah as they walked home. *Home.* She'd never thought to see this modest house again. Rand laughed as he tried to tell their story. But the true story still had to be told.

Amelia sent Joel out with the men, then heated a kettle of water and poured it into a hip bath as Sarah peeled off the dusty, stained buckskin dress. She poured cold water into the bath and tested to make sure it wasn't too hot, then as Sarah eased in with a sigh, Amelia began to comb the tangles out of her friend's red-gold locks.

A half hour later, hair washed and clad in clean clothes, Sarah curled up on the sofa while Amelia stood over her, plaiting Sarah's hair into a long braid. "You have so many bruises. But of course the Indians are notorious for their brutality."

Her friend's sympathetic touch and voice broke the dam on Sarah's emotions, and she burst into tears. She had to tell someone—she couldn't hold it inside any longer. "It wasn't the Indians, Amelia—they helped me. It was Ben."

Amelia's fingers in Sarah's hair stilled. "Ben Croftner? He beat you?" Her voice was incredulous, and she curled her hands into fists.

Sarah nodded. In a flood, the horror of her ordeal gushed out. Amelia sat and held her as she choked out the truth.

"Did you tell Rand?" White with shock and disbelief, Amelia pushed the hair out of Sarah's face, then held her close again.

"No. But I know I have to." Sarah pulled back and laced her hands together. "I–I just couldn't face it. He'll hate me, I know it. You know how jealous he is of Ben." She shuddered. "What if he thinks I encouraged him? What if he doesn't believe me when I tell him I got away before Ben could—?"

The words hung in the air. Amelia placed her hand over Sarah's hands. "Oh, Sarah, he'll believe you. He's learned to trust again these last few months. And I'm sure he doesn't blame you anymore. It wasn't your fault."

The front door banged open, and they both turned as Rand, Joel, and Jacob strode into the room.

Rand's face brightened when he saw Sarah. "You look much better."

"Well, I'm starved. How 'bout you, honey?" Jacob pulled Amelia to her feet. "Let's go get some grub at the mess hall." They started toward the door. "Come with us, half-pint," he told Joel. "We won't be late," he called over his shoulder.

The ploy to leave them alone was too obvious to be missed, and Sarah suppressed a smile. "I'll fix you some flapjacks." Rand stared at her arm, and she pulled her shawl over the bruises there.

"I'm not hungry yet. We need to talk. I want to know what happened. You've been avoiding my questions. And I have some things to tell you too."

Sarah sat back down abruptly. She was tired of worrying about his reaction. There was only one way to find out. "I was afraid you'd blame me, but I swear to you I had no idea he would try something like that."

"Who are you talking about?"

"Ben. He hired some Laramie loafers to grab me," she blurted the words out in a rush, then hurried on as his face darkened. "When I came to, I was in a locked cabin by myself. Ben showed up—" She drew a ragged breath. "He—he said we should have been married by then. He . . ." Her words trailed away at the irate expression on his face.

"That no-good skunk. So that's what he meant." Rand leaned over and touched her arm. "He gave you those bruises? Did he—did he hurt you in any other way?"

She shook her head. "I hit him over the head with a stool leg and knocked him out cold. Then I took off and got away while he was out. Labe was there too, but he wasn't watching the cabin. What did you mean, 'that's what he meant'? When did you talk to him?"

Rand drew a couple of deep breaths, then grabbed his hat.

"Where are you going?"

"To find Jessica. I have some unfinished business to take care of." He came back and kissed her quickly. "Don't go outside the grounds. I might not be lucky enough to find you a second time. Don't look so worried. I'll tell the whole story when I get back." He gazed down into her eyes, then stroked her cheek. "I know it wasn't your fault, Green Eyes."

She watched him go with some relief. He did trust her after all. "Be careful," she called after his retreating back.

Jessica looked up as her mother ushered Rand into the parlor, then left them alone. "Darling." She rose to her feet. "I didn't know you were back." She lifted her face for a kiss, but Rand just stared at her impassively. "What is it? What's wrong?"

"Your little plan failed."

"Whatever do you mean?" Her blue eyes looked huge and innocent.

Rand could see behind her beauty now. She was like a snake, gorgeous coloring but a deadly bite. "I know all about it, Jessica. Ben told me the whole story when he tried to kill me."

Her eyes widened. "Ben who? Who tried to kill you?"

Rand could see the pulse beating quickly in her throat. She was a smooth one all right. "You and Ben schemed to kidnap Sarah to get her away from me. You knew I still loved her. Don't bother to deny it. And it almost worked. But I found her, and we pieced together what the two of you cooked up between you."

Jessica's face whitened. "How could you prefer that little milksop to me?" She put her hand to her mouth, and her eyes filled with tears. "I love you, Rand. I didn't want to lose you. Surely you can see I had to do something. I could see the hold she had over you."

"I love her. I always have." He saw her flinch but went on anyway. "I tried to deceive myself, but I can't any longer. How could you do such a thing? If people just knew the evil that hides behind that beautiful mask of yours! You can consider our engagement off, of course." He put his hat on and stalked toward the door.

"Wait, Rand!" Jessica ran after him and caught his sleeve. "I know you love me. We can work this out."

He shook her hand off. "All I feel for you is contempt." He didn't wait to see the effect of his words but slammed the door behind him.

That was over. Now to find Croftner. He stopped to see the colonel, who readily agreed to let him take six men out to look for Ben and try to bring him in.

After two days Rand had no luck in picking up Ben's trail. Reluctantly, he turned toward Fort Laramie and home. He hated to face Sarah with his failure. Neither one of them could rest until they knew the threat Ben posed was eliminated.

He paused atop a bluff, took a swig from his canteen, then led the men down the slope. "Lieutenant, over here!" One of the men waved from the top of the bluff.

Rand trotted over to where the men stood. A body lay facedown in a ravine. He rolled the man over and gasped. It was Labe. He groaned, and Rand turned to hail one of his men. "Get me my canteen." He poured a little water into Labe's mouth. "Easy, now. Not too much," he cautioned as Labe tried to sit up to suck more water down.

"Indians!" Labe moaned and thrashed around as Rand drew the canteen away.

"They're gone. You're with friends now."

"Rand?" Labe peered up at him. "I'm sorry 'bout poor little Sarah. I tried to talk Ben out of it, but he wouldn't listen to no reason."

"Where is Ben?"

Tears welled up in Labe's eyes. "Dead. Indians attacked us. Ben fought them, but he fell off his horse and hit his head. "I–I buried him over there." He pointed to a long pile of rocks.

Rand patted his shoulder. "How'd you get away?"

"They left me here." He touched his head gingerly. "They must have hit me on the head."

"You'll be all right. We just need to get you back to the fort." He helped Labe to his feet and helped him up into the saddle. It was a long way back to Fort Laramie.

The week flew by as Sarah immersed herself in activity. She tried to still the worry as she thought of Rand out looking for Ben. On Monday, Wednesday, and Friday morning she taught the Indian children. Living with the Sioux for those four days gave her a new love and tenderness for the dark-eyed youngsters who crowded into the small church. She delighted in seeing their solemn faces break into smile.

She had just gotten back from school when Joel burst into the parlor. "Rand's back!" She jumped to her feet and followed him onto the porch where she saw a familiar set of broad shoulders striding toward her across the parade ground. With a cry, she ran into his open arms.

He hugged her tightly, then led her back inside the house. Joel jabbered excitedly as he followed them. "I need to talk to your sister for a few minutes alone, half-pint. Can you find something else to do for a little while?"

"Sure. Tommy Justice, the new lieutenant's son, said he'd play baseball with me."

"Thanks." Rand turned back to Sarah. "Sit down

here with me. We have a lot to talk about." He took her hand.

Sarah sat beside him, her heart pounding at his solemn face.

"Ben's dead." He told her what Labe had told him and then the entire story of Ben's plot.

Sarah was surprised at her own reaction. She felt unexplainable sadness over Ben's wasted life, although he had received his just reward. "I read a verse this morning. It said, 'And he shall bring upon them their own iniquity, and shall cut them off in their own wickedness; yea, the Lord our God shall cut them off.'"

Rand nodded. "But Jessica was in on it too. And God hasn't cut her off."

She squeezed his hand as the words sank in. "That was the plan I heard them talking about."

He nodded again. "The whole thing was her idea." He raked a hand through his dark hair. "Not that Ben wouldn't have come up with something himself."

"Why would she do such a thing?"

"To get you away from me." He stared into her face. "She sensed I still had feelings for you." He shook his head. "I had no idea she was capable of such an act of vengeance."

Her heart surged at his admission in spite of her shock. He did still love her. "That's why she left Fort Laramie in such a hurry." She saw his questioning look. "She left the day after you did. She's going to Boston with her mother."

"I see." He took a deep breath. "I wanted to tell you at the Sioux encampment, but I felt it was only right that I break things off with Jessica first. I've been a fool, Sarah. I never stopped loving you. I've never loved anyone but you."

She laid a hand on his cheek. "There's nothing to forgive. I've always loved you."

He caught her hand and brought her palm to his lips. "Will you marry me?"

"When?" Her stomach was playing mumblety-peg as he kissed her palm lingeringly.

"Today wouldn't be too soon." He put an arm around her and pulled her onto his lap. "I love you so much, Green Eyes. Even when I told myself I hated you, deep down I knew better." He traced a finger along the curve of her smooth cheek, then bent his head.

As his lips found hers, tears slipped out of Sarah's eyes. She put her arms around his neck as the kiss became more urgent. When he pulled away, she slid her fingers through the rough thatch of his hair.

"Let's not wait too long to marry," he whispered. "I want you all to myself."

"Me too," she said, blushing. "But what about Joel?"

"He'll live with us, of course. I love him like a brother. But I think Jacob will keep him for a week or so while we settle into married life."

She'd known he loved Joel, but it soothed her to hear him say the words. She nestled her face against his shirt.

EPILOGUE

A crisp spring morning three days later, Sarah and Rand stood before the post chaplain, Reverend Jameson. Every soldier in the fort had crammed into the tiny church to see their girl decked out in her finery.

In the front pew their families smiled as they watched them say their vows. Joel had been ecstatic when he'd realized he'd get to live with Rand.

After Rand and Sarah repeated their promises, the men behind them put up a rousing cheer as Rand, in his best uniform, kissed Sarah and turned to face the crowd. The officers formed a canopy of swords that he led his bride through and out into the spring sunshine.

Sarah wore her mama's green dress, a perfect match for the emerald eyes she raised to Rand as they clasped hands and stepped out to meet their new life together. Her heart had truly led her home.

A JOURNEY of the HEART

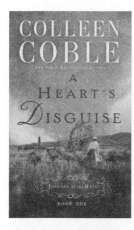

COLLEEN COBLE

A HEART'S DISGUISE

BOOK ONE

COLLEEN COBLE

A HEART'S OBSESSION

BOOK TWO

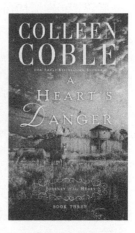

COLLEEN COBLE

A HEART'S DANGER

BOOK THREE

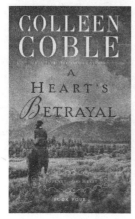

COLLEEN COBLE

A HEART'S BETRAYAL

BOOK FOUR

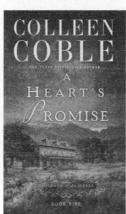

COLLEEN COBLE

A HEART'S PROMISE

BOOK FIVE

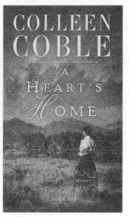

COLLEEN COBLE

A HEART'S HOME

BOOK SIX

AVAILABLE IN PRINT STARTING MARCH 2015

THOMAS NELSON
Since 1798

9780529103413-A

A vacation to Sunset Cove was her way of celebrating and thanking her parents. After all, Claire Dellamore's childhood was like a fairytale. But with the help of Luke Elwell, Claire discovers that fairytale was really an elaborate lie . . .

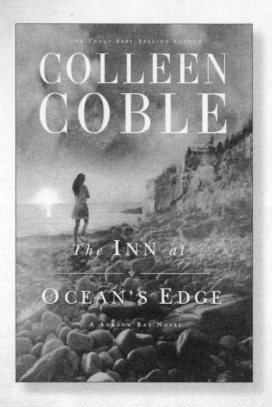

ESCAPE TO BLUEBIRD RANCH

AVAILABLE IN PRINT AND E-BOOK

THOMAS NELSON
Since 1798

Colleen loves to hear from her readers!

Be sure to sign up for Colleen's newsletter for insider information on deals and appearances.

Visit her website at www.colleencoble.com
Twitter: @colleencoble
Facebook: colleencoblebooks

THOMAS NELSON
Since 1798

About the Author

R ITA finalist Colleen Coble is the author of several bestselling romantic suspense novels, including *Tidewater Inn*, and the Mercy Falls, Lonestar, and Rock Harbor series.